Prophets of Islam
Children Book 2

Akhtar A. Alvi, P.E.

Razia Akhtar Alvi Institute
For
Empowering Studies Lahore,
Pakistan

Prophets of Islam - Children Book Of Islam 2

CONTENTS

ALVI FAMILY PORTRAIT – 1983	4
DEDICATION	5
ACKNOWLEDGMENT	6
CHAPTER 1 WHY WRITE THIS BOOK?	7
CHAPTER 2 WHO IS PROPHET OF ISLAM?	8
CHAPTER 3 ROLE MODEL	9
CHAPTER 4 PROPHET'S BIRTH AND DEATH	13
CHAPTER 5 PROPHET'S FAMILY	17
CHAPTER 6 PROPHET'S MARRIAGES AND CHILDREN	19
CHAPTER 7 PROPHET'S LIFE AND CAREER	23
CHAPTER 8 PROPHET'S WAY OF LIFE	26
AUTHOR	29

COPYRIGHT © 2025

PROPHETS OF ISLAM BY
AKHTAR A. ALVI, P.E.

eBook ISBN: 978-1-967106-92-9
Paperback ISBN: 978-1-967106-93-6
Hardcover ISBN: 978-1-967106-94-3

All rights are reserved. No part of this book may be used or reproduced by any means, graphic, electronic, or mechanical, including photocopying, recording, taping or by any information storage retrieval system without the written permission of the author except in the case of brief quotations embodied in critical articles and reviews.

This book is sold subject to the conditions that it shall not, by way of trade or otherwise, be lent, re-sold, hired out or otherwise circulated without the author's prior consent in any form of binding or cover other than that in which it is published.

Prophets of Islam - Children Book Of Islam

ALVI FAMILY PORTRAIT – 1983

- Back: Left to right - Razia, Akhtar.
- Front: Anwar, Rizwan (elder son).
- Immigrated to the USA, 1976.
- Anwar was 6-week, and Rizwan was 20 ½ months old.

DEDICATION

I dedicate this book to my late family members:

- Spouse: Razia A. Alvi.
- Grandparents:

> Maternal: Zainab Bibi and Wali Muhammad.
> Paternal: Jivi Bibi and Khushi Muhammad.

- Parents: Barkat Bibi and Hakim Muhammad Hussain Alvi.
- In–Laws: Chirag Bibi Shah and Rahmat Ullah Shah.
- Auntie and Uncle: Sardaran Begum and Subedar- Major Haji Ali Muhammad Alvi.
- Paternal Auntie: Beernisan Bibi.
- Brothers: Anwar, Sarwar, and Zafar.
- Sister: Kishwar.
- Cousin: Rashid Ahmad, Dilbar Hussain, Suria and Rakia
- Brother-in-Law: Hashmat Shah.
- Sister-in-Laws: Ulfat and Bushra.

God please bless their souls and reward them paradise.

ACKNOWLEDGMENT

Thanks to:

- Google and Wikipedia for use of their material.
- Aisha Junaid for her editing and additions.
- Elisa Coleman and her team at Turner Publishing for publishing, marketing and selling the book worldwide.
- Dr. Kamran and his staff at the Legacy Venture International, Lahore, Pakistan, for promoting the book in Pakistan and worldwide.

CHAPTER 1

WHY WRITE THIS BOOK?

During the 980s, I performed community service at the Islamic Society of Greater Houston's (ISGH's) North Zone/Bilal Mosque. I was the founding Editor-in-Chief of its magazine, Al-Qaasid, from February 1987 to April 1988. At that time, I drafted this book, but could not publish it.

My purpose of writing this book is to teach children the principles of Islam. The life of Prophet Muhammad is the best example for humans. Through this book, I am introducing you to his character.

You will learn:

- Who he was and why he is the best example for humanity.
- The key events of his life from his birth to the passing away.
- His family, marriages, and relationship with children.
- The principles and lifestyle he embodied, which continue to guide us today.

The teachings of Prophet Muhammad were not limited to a specific time or place. They are for every era and all ages. His simplicity, morals, and principles of love remain a path to peace and harmony in the world today.

This book will not only enhance your knowledge but also inspire you to become a better person by following his teachings. It is my heartfelt wish that, through this book, you learn about Prophet Muhammad, strive to improve your life, and show kindness and good behavior toward others.

CHAPTER 2

WHO IS PROPHET OF ISLAM?

Prophet Muhammad is the messenger of Islam, chosen by God to guide humanity. One of his names is Ahmad, which means "the praised one." God has honored the Prophet in the Quran and commanded believers to send blessings upon him:

"May God's peace and blessings be upon Prophet Muhammad (peace be upon him."

Prophet Muhammad was born in the city of Makkah in the Quraysh tribe. Tragically, his father passed away before his birth, and his mother died when he was six years old. He was cared for by his grandfather and later by his uncle.

From a young age, Prophet Muhammad was known for his truthfulness, honesty, and compassion. People called him As-Sadiq (the truthful) and Al-Amin (the trustworthy).

The primary goal of his life was to call people to worship God and teach them good character and love for one another. He was a gentle, kind, and compassionate person.

CHAPTER 3

ROLE MODEL

He:

- He never lied.
- He always helped others, especially those in need.
- He was incredibly loving and kind toward children.

Through this book, you will learn how the principles of the Prophet Muhammad's life can guide us to become better individuals.

The Placement of the Black Stone (Hajr-e-Aswad)

Masjid Al Haram

The life of Prophet Muhammad is filled with many interesting and valuable lessons. One such story is about the placement of the Black Stone (Hajr-e-Aswad) at the Kaaba / Grand mosque in Makkah. It teaches children the importance of unity, wisdom, and fairness

Prophets of Islam - Children Book Of Islam

When Prophet Muhammad was a young man, the Kaaba was being reconstructed. When the time came to place the sacred Black Stone in its position, a dispute arose among the tribes. Each tribe wanted the honor of placing the stone, and the disagreement escalated to the point where a fight seemed inevitable.

To resolve the matter, the tribes decided that the first person to enter the Kaaba the next morning would make the final decision. By God's will, Prophet Muhammad was the first to arrive. Known for his honesty and wisdom, he was trusted by everyone and called Al-Amin (the trustworthy).

The Prophet proposed a fair and intelligent solution. He asked for a large cloth to be brought and placed the Black Stone in its center. Then, he invited the leaders of all the tribes to hold the corners of the cloth together and lift it. Once the stone was near its designated spot, Prophet

Muhammad personally placed it in position with his own hands.

Lessons from the Incident

- Unity Matters: Challenges can be resolved by working together.
- Wisdom and Justice: A wise decision can end conflicts and

- **Respect for Others:** Giving everyone an opportunity and involving all parties fosters harmony.

make everyone happy.

This story is not only inspiring but also teaches essential values for life.

The Compassionate Camel

One day, Prophet was walking through the streets of Medina when he saw a camel that looked sad. It was sitting in a corner, and tears were streaming from its eyes. The Prophet went to the camel, placed his hand on its head, and spoke to it softly. The camel became calm.

The Prophet asked: Whose camel is this? A young man stepped forward and said: O Messenger of God, this camel belongs to me. The Prophet said: This camel is complaining that you overwork it and do not give it enough food and rest. Treat this creature of God with kindness.

Hearing this, the young man felt ashamed and promised to take good care of the camel.

Lesson

This story teaches us to treat animals with kindness and love. They are creations of God. It is our responsibility to take care of them; as Prophet Muhammad did.

A Bird's Nest

One day, Prophet Muhammad was traveling with his companions. They made a stop under a tree. Some of the companions went near the tree and saw a bird's nest with two baby birds inside.

Out of curiosity, one of them picked up the baby birds. As this happened, the mother bird became distressed and started flying around the nest, making loud cries. When Prophet Muhammad saw this, he immediately said: "Who has separated these baby birds from their mother? Look how anxious she is. Return them at once!"

The companions quickly returned the baby birds to the nest. The mother bird, relieved, flew back to her young ones.

Lesson

A mother's love is unconditional compassionate love. No matter the mother is a human, an animal or a bird. It is like God's love for humans. In Arabic, He is called Ar-Rahman.

CHAPTER 4

PROPHET'S BIRTH AND DEATH

Prophet Mohammad was born:

- ➤ In the city of Mecca, Saudi Arabia.
- ➤ On April 20, 571.

Prophet Mohammad Died on 8 June 8, 632 in Medina.

Birth

When he was born, his grandfather, Abdul Muttalib, named him "Muhammad," which means "the praised one." This name, rare at the time, later became famous worldwide.

Prophet Muhammad's father was Abdullah, and his mother was Amina. His father had passed away before his birth, and he entered the world as an orphan.

At the time of his birth, Makkah was steeped in idol worship, but God had chosen Prophet Muhammad to deliver the message of the oneness of God and to guide humanity away from moral corruption.

Childhood

Prophet Muhammad faced many hardships during his early years. At the age of six, his mother passed away, and his grandfather, Abdul Muttalib, took care of him. When the Prophet was eight years old, his grandfather also passed away, and his uncle, Abu Talib, assumed responsibility for his upbringing.

Passing Away

Prophet Muhammad passed away on June 8, 632 CE, in Madinah at the age of 63. His passing was a great loss for the Muslim community. However, he left behind a way of life that serves as guidance for humanity until the Day of Judgment.

His Legacy

Despite his departure, the teachings of Prophet Muhammad – the Quran and his Sunnah/Sayings – continue to guide us on how to lead a meaningful and successful life in this world and the hereafter. Every moment of his life is a lesson for both children and adults, and this is why he is known as "Rahmatul-Lil-Alameen" (Mercy for the universe).

CHAPTER 5

PROPHET'S FAMILY

Prophet Muhammad was born in the Quraysh tribe. It was one of the respected tribes of Mecca.

In his early years, God put him through many trials, but each trial strengthened his character and made him even more remarkable. These experiences laid the foundation for his patience, gratitude, and noble character.

The details of his family are:

His:

- Mother was Amina.
- Father was Abdullah.
- Grandfather was Abdul Muttalib.
- Father passed away before his birth.
- Mother passed away when he was six years old.
- Grandfather looked after him. But he passed away when he was eight years old. Then his uncle Abu Talib looked after him. He was his favorite uncle.

Nursing:

According to the Meccan tradition, Prophet Muhammad was sent to a rural woman, Halimah Saadiyah. She breastfed him and took care of him. His presence, in her household, brought God's blessings on the family.

Mother:

His mother's name was Amina bint Wahb. She was from the Banu Zuhrah tribe. She was a noble and virtuous woman. Prophet

Muhammad always had love and affection for his mother in his heart.

- His mother, Amina, passed away when he was only six years old. This was a huge shock for him.

Father:

His father's name was Abdullah ibn Abdul Muttalib, one of the respected members of the Quraysh tribe. His father passed away before his birth, leaving him an orphan.

Grandfather:

His grandfather's name was Abdul Muttalib. He was the chief of the Quraysh tribe. He took on the responsibility of raising Prophet Muhammad with love and compassion. Abdul Muttalib considered his birth to be a blessing from God and named him "Muhammad," which means "the praised one." But he too passed away when Prophet Muhammad was eight years old.

Siblings:

Prophet Muhammad had no sisters and brothers. He was an only child, but close relatives and uncles played an important role in his life.

Uncles:

He had eight uncles, of whom Abu Talib played a key role in his upbringing. Abu Talib was not only his guardian but also loved him dearly and always supported him, no matter the circumstances. He was like a father to Prophet.

CHAPTER 6

PROPHET'S MARRIAGES AND CHILDREN

Prophet Muhammad married 13 women. These marriages took place for social and humanitarian reasons. Through these marriages, he promoted important objectives such as social reform, unity among tribes, and helping the weak.

Spouse	Married
1. Khadija	595–619
2. Sawdah	619–632
3. Aisha	623–632
4. Hafsah	625–632

5.	Zaynab bint Khuzayma	625–626
6.	Hind	625–632
7.	Zaynab bint Jahsh	627–632
8.	Juwayriya	628–632
9.	Ramla	628–632
10.	Safiyya	629–632
11.	Maymunah	629–632
12.	Rayhanah	627–631
13.	Mariyya	628–632

Detail:

Prophet Muhammad's first wife was Khadija. She was a rich business woman. She used all her wealth in spreading the message of Islam alongside the Prophet. She remained his only wife until her death in 619. It ended their 24-year marriage. With the exception of Aisha, all of the women were widowed or divorced.

All but two of his marriages were contracted after this migration from Mecca to Madinah.

After the passing of Khadijah, the Prophet married Sawda, who was a widow. The purpose of this marriage was to provide for her.

Aisha, the daughter of Prophet's friend Abu Bakr, was the Prophet's only virgin wife. Their marriage was aimed at strengthening ties with the Quraysh tribe. Aisha was very intelligent and played a key role in advancing the teachings of Islam.

Hafsa, the daughter of Umar al-Farooq, married the Prophet after she became a widow.

Zaynab, a widow known as "Umm al-Masakin" (Mother of the Poor), married the Prophet one year before her death. She was a cousin of the Prophet. She married him as part of a social reform.

She was married to Prophet Muhammad's adopted son, who was a black slave.

Hind, known as Umm Salama, was also a widow. The marriage was made to provide for her children.

Juwayriya was from the Banu Mustaliq tribe. After their marriage, many members of her tribe embraced Islam.

Ramlah, known as Umm Habiba, was a widow, and the marriage was aimed at improving relations with the Quraysh.

Safiyya came from a Jewish tribe. After their marriage, the relationship between Muslims and Jews improved.

Maymunah married the Prophet after her family embraced Islam.

Raihana was from a Jewish tribe but later accepted Islam. Her marriage to the Prophet was brief.

Maria al-Qibtiyya came from Egypt as a gift and accepted Islam. She gave birth to a son, Ibrahim, who passed away.

Prophet Muhammad had seven children (three sons and four daughters). All but one of them was from Khadija. Mariyya bore Prophet Muhammad a son in 630. But none of his sons survived to adulthood.

Children

Qasim (598–601)
Zainab (599–629)
Ruqayya (601–624)
Umm Kulthum (603–630)
Fatima (605–632)
Abd Allah (611–615)
Ibrahim (630–632)

Prophet Muhammad had seven children, three sons and four daughters. All but one of them, Ibrahim, was with Khadija. Mariyya bore Muhammad a son in 630, but none of his sons survived.

Fatima was married to Prophet Muhammad's cousin, They five children; two girls, **Zainab** and **Umm-e-Kulthum,** and three boys, Mohsin, who died in infancy, Hassan and Hussain.

CHAPTER 7

PROPHET'S LIFE AND CAREER

The life of Prophet Muhammad can be divided into two periods:

1. Before the Migration (Makkah, 570-622). This period covers events from his birth to the migration to Madinah.
2. Migration to Madinah.

He was born in 570 CE in Makkah. During his youth, he gained fame for his honesty and truthfulness and became known as "As-Sadiq" (The Truthful) and "Al-Amin" (The Trustworthy).

- Beginning of Prophethood: In 610 CE, he received the first revelation in the Cave of Hira, where God appointed him as His Prophet. After that, he began inviting people to Islam, initially in secret, and later openly.

- Challenges during the Makkah Period: During this time, the disbelievers of Makkah opposed Islam and persecuted the Muslims. The Prophet continued his mission with patience and wisdom, encouraging his followers to remain steadfast in their faith.

After the Migration to Madinah (622-632):

After the migration (Hijrah) to Madinah, a new chapter of the Prophet's life began.

- The Meaning of Hijrah: The Hijrah is the migration of Prophet Muhammad and the early Muslims from Makkah to Madinah.

- This step was taken to escape the oppression of the disbelievers of Makkah and establish a free Islamic state. The Hijrah is a significant milestone in Islamic history, and the

Islamic calendar (Hijri) begins with this event.

- The Islamic State of Madinah: Upon arriving in Madinah, the Prophet established an organized society for the Muslims. Through the "Constitution of Madinah," he laid down the principles of peaceful coexistence with Jews, Christians, and other tribes.

- Worship and Teachings: During this period, many important Islamic laws were revealed, including the prayers (Salah), alms (Zakat), fasting (Sawm), and pilgrimage (Hajj).

- The Last Ten Years (622-632): During the last ten years of his life, several important campaigns and battles took place, aimed at defending Islam and struggling against oppression.

Battles Against the Quraysh.

- Battle of Badr (624):

This was the first major battle, where the Muslims achieved victory with the help of Allah.

- Battle of Uhud (625:

In this battle, the Muslims suffered a temporary setback, but it did not result in a significant advantage for the Quraysh.

- Battle of the Trench (627)

This was a defensive battle against the Quraysh and their allies, where the Muslims successfully defended Madinah by digging a trench.

- Conquest of Makkah (629)

After years of opposition, Makkah was conquered in 629 CE without major bloodshed. Following this event, the people of Makkah embraced Islam, and the Ka'bah was cleansed of idol.

Campaigns against the Jewish Tribes

- After agreements with the three Jewish tribes of Madinah (Banu Qaynuqa, Banu Nadir, and Banu Qurayza) and their violations of the agreements, the Prophet led campaigns against them.

- Battle of Khaybar (628)

A successful campaign was launched against the Jewish forts in Khaybar, resulting in a Muslim victory.

Ethical Principles

In all these wars and campaigns, Prophet Muhammad always upheld human rights, compassion, and justice. He treated even his enemies with kindness and pardoned prisoners of war.

These two periods of Prophet Muhammad's life teach us lessons of patience, sacrifice, and struggle, which continue to guide us today.

CHAPTER 8

PROPHET'S WAY OF LIFE

The way of life is conduct, character and personality. Conduct is behaving with others based on moral principles. Character:

- Refers to a person's moral and ethical qualities.
- Consists of beliefs and moral principles that guide behavior.

Personality is:

- The sum of a person's physical, psychological, emotional, and social aspects.
- Behavior and actions.

Prophet Muhammad:

- Had no schooling.
- Was the educator who was never ashamed to say: I don't know.
- Was:

➤ A good boy.
➤ Called Al-Sadiq meaning he always spoke the truth.
➤ A very generous person. He helped the poor and the needy.

- Never:

➤ Said a bad word.
➤ Fight with anyone.
➤ Told a lie.

- Liked simple food. He loved dates, milk and watermelon. He ate whatever was given to him and thanked God.

- Spoke politely. He never shouted and lost his temper. He forgave his enemies.
- Helped the family. He kindled the fire; swept the floor; milked the sheep; and mended his shoes and garments. In other words, he not only endured the coarseness of an austere life, but it came naturally to him.
- Loved children. He played with them. He carried them on his back and gave them rides on his camel. He told them stories.
- One day he played with a little girl, Umm Khalid. He did not forget her. Later he gave her a gift of a lovely shawl. She was very happy.
- Helped others. One day Adhan was called for prayer. Suddenly a man rushed to the Prophet and said that he had difficulty in finishing his work. Prophet went to help him. Then he came back to say the prayer.

God revealed the Quran to Prophet Muhammad to guide the humans. He was a practical example to follow the Quran's teachings to believe in the oneness of God, do good deeds by helping humans, and avoiding sins.

Prophet Muhammad was God's last messenger. God made him prophet at age 40.

Prophet Muhammad preached and practiced love and peace at all levels: personal, domestic, social, inter-religious and international. He implemented the Qur'an's teaching that interfaith dialogue should be based on persuasion and wisdom, and not through confrontational use of force. In his famous last sermon, delivered at the sacred occasion of Hajj, only three months before his passing away, he said:

Your lives and possessions have been made immune by God to attacks by one another until the Day of Judgment…All humans are equal to one another…An Arab has no superiority over a non-Arab, or a non- Arab over an Arab; nor a white one be preferred to a dark one, nor a dark one to a white one…You are all brothers, so be not divided! God has made the life, property and honor of every one sacred!

Historian Michael H. Hart, in his ranking of the 100 most influential persons in history, has ranked Prophet Muhammad as #1.

His clansmen had officially titled him *al-Amin* (the Trustworthy). Meccans wanted to kill him. He was hiding in a cave. There he instructed his cousin Ali to stay behind in Mecca, to return all the property the Messenger of Allah had held in trust for people.

The Prophet's character was the Qur'an, as described by his wife, Aisha. He practiced everything that he preached, and since the Qur'anic message preached mercy above all. This quality was more pronounced in his practice than anything else.

Quraysh spared no opportunity to demonize him. They divorced his daughters, and they starved his entire clan for three years which led to the death of his wife and his most supportive uncle.

AUTHOR

Akhtar A. Alvi, P.E., is:

- An International Management Consultant.
- A retired Civil and Environmental Engineer, and a Project Manager.
- A U.S. citizen of Pakistani heritage.

He:

- Earned a Bachelor of Science and two Master of Science degrees in Civil Engineering from the University Of Engineering & Technology, Lahore, Pakistan, and the Louisiana State University, Baton Rouge, Louisiana, USA.
- Taught Civil Engineering at the University of Engineering and Technology, Lahore, and Louisiana State University.
- Developed irrigation and hydropower projects for the Government of Nigeria and managed engineering and environmental projects for oil and gas companies in the United States and for the U.S. government.
- Mr. Alvi is the author of multiple books, which are available at Amazon.com

Made in the USA
Monee, IL
22 May 2025

17665615R00019